The
Scarlet Destruction

S.L. Baron

The Scarlet Destruction

Print Edition ISBN: 978-1-7345598-1-1

Author's Note

This is intended for mature audiences, as it contains harsh language and sexual encounters. It also addresses sensitive topics including race, violence, war, religion, suicide, and rape. Parts are influenced by events that took place in the United States in 2014. The events have been fictionalized but have the potential to make some readers uncomfortable.

Acknowledgements

First, a huge thank you to Tim for putting up with me through this entire process. His support and willingness to let me sequester myself in the office to write and edit and to randomly rant about the writing process is appreciated more than I can express to him.

Thank you to Robert Tomoguchi, K.V. Wilson, and Jimmie Bise, Junior, who support me as patrons on Patreon. I love having them on this creative journey with me!

Also By The Author

Vanilla Blood: A Novella
Blood Ties
"Effing Dave"
One Million Project Fantasy Anthology

The Scarlet Destruction

One

"I know you want to ask me if I need a donut, don't deny it."

Fiona stared, trying hard not to drop the hazelnut macchiato she just topped off.

It was one thing to dream about people who came into the Purple Bear—who didn't dream about their jobs? —but when those people said the exact thing to you in waking life… now, that went too far in her opinion.

She set the coffee down. "Wouldn't that be a bit rude to say to an officer of the law?" Fiona tilted her head to the side and folded her arms over the swell of her breasts.

The words "West Virginia State Police" raised as his muscular shoulders lifted into a shrug. "Meh. I've heard worse." A voice crackled over his radio. He grabbed the cup and headed for the door, throwing her a quick glance and tipping his wide-brimmed cap.

The barista watched until his dark blue and gold Chevy Impala disappeared, then sat down on the stool behind the counter. It was the first time the state trooper said more than an order to her, and it went exactly like the dream.

"Just breathe, Fiona," she mumbled. "Merely an odd coincidence."

"What's that, Fi?" Jaime popped out from the kitchen. "Was that Hot Cop I heard out here?"

She killed him with a cerulean look. For a month, they had tried to covertly admire the man's good looks.

"It was! Oh, how you'd love to take him out of that sexy forest-green uniform. Hell, *I* wouldn't mind taking him out of that uniform, but he'd probably shoot my ass. And, sadly, not in the way I want."

She gave him a sideways glance. Even after knowing him for eight years, hearing her friend and boss lust after men was sometimes odd. Jaime Hess's six-foot, muscular frame and cropped, blonde beard exuded classic masculinity, but he never minded telling her how his picture could be found in the gay dictionary under "bear."

The pastry chef lightly punched her on the shoulder. "Damn. You're shaking. Ya all right?" An eyebrow raised in concern.

Fiona Albright inhaled, her Titian ponytail bobbing. "Yeah. Yeah, of course!" She laughed. "It was the first time he said more than a coffee order to me. Made me all weak in the knees."

"Getting all nervous schoolgirl on me? For shame!" Jaime shook his head and returned to the kitchen as a group of college-aged hipsters entered the shop. "Ohhh. Have fun! Looks like we're gonna run out of soy milk."

"You know they'd stop coming in here if you'd stop wearing flannel." Jaime raised a hand above his head to flip her off. Fiona rolled her eyes. "*Fucking* hipsters. I fucking hate hipsters," she said under her breath.

꙰

The sound of waves breaking met Fiona's ears, but the fog around her was so thick, all she could see were varying shades of white: grayish-white sky above; pale pearl-white sand under her bare feet; foamy white crests breaking in front of her.

Warm water lapped up her bare legs as she walked forward. She closed her eyes with a moan as the gentle waves moved up her midriff. Then, like every night, she let the current pull her under.

꙰

A lush walled garden surrounded her when she opened her eyes.

Fiona turned around slowly, taking in the vibrant green of the leaves and the brightly colored flowers. Vermillion roses bordered the path she followed to a swing. She swung a moment, breathing in the fragrance of lilacs and gardenias.

"Mmm, *Syringa vulgaris* and *Gardenia jasminoides*," she reminisced, the Latin names tumbling off her tongue with the same ease they had ten years prior. "If I only had made it to school for botany." A sigh left her. "There's something more for me here than just my favorite flowers, though." Hopping from the wooden seat, she studied the forked path in front of her. "Let's try right."

Fiona didn't think twice about how unusual her dream life was. Lucid dreams were her norm, though she kept the fact to herself. When people told her about their odd, sometimes frightening, dreams, she couldn't fathom not having control over actions in her own. *Luckily, not all of them end up overlapping the waking world.*

She ended up at a wrought iron bench, tucked her feet under herself, and picked up the leather-bound tome beside her. Though the language looked alien, her brain had no problem understanding the writing: an epic poem about two spirits in human form, brought together by a group of religious fanatics.

"Why is this so familiar?"

Fiona paused, the feeling of eyes suddenly on her. Her "hot cop" leaned against the stone wall in uniform pants and a white t-shirt, watching her. A musical chuckle bounced off the stone walls. "Caught me." His amber eyes glinted playfully. "I do enjoy watching an intelligent woman read." A corner of his full lips lifted. "You pout in the prettiest way when you do, Fiona."

She closed the book, placing it carefully next to her. Her lips pursed, and her head tilted to study him. The slight cockiness in the way he held himself was annoyingly attractive. "I've had you in my dreams quite a bit lately. It's a bit embarrassing, really, considering I don't even know your name."

He smiled as he walked toward her and knelt on one knee in front of the bench. "You do know my name. You made yourself forget."

"Do I?" She bit her lip as she thought hard. "Why would I want to forget?" Her brow furrowed as she met his eyes.

He seemed at a loss for words. "Because forgetting was what you wanted. We both have at times, but you managed it somehow." His gaze moved away from hers. "You're the clever one. Sometimes, I think you *like* to make it difficult on me." He gently grasped her hands; her fingertips tingled as he kissed them softly. "Let me help you remember. My name is Gabriel. Gabe, preferably."

Fiona laughed. "Gabe, of course! What else have I forgotten?"

Gabe bowed his head. "So very much, Fiona. But you *need* to remember and soon. It's gotten bad. We've let it go too long." He stood up, releasing her hands. "We'll talk soon, though. There's not enough time right now. We both need to go to work." He walked away.

Fiona snapped awake and glanced at the clock, groaning. "Time to go make lattes. Yay."

⌘

The afternoon proved painfully slow. Jaime used the downtime to meticulously scrub the already spotless kitchen. A lone patron sat in the back, typing furiously on a laptop. Fiona entertained herself with a Terry Pratchett book, pausing at times to mourn the author's recent death.

She took pause as the nagging feeling of being watched crept over her. The barista nearly fell off the stool as she met the trooper's silent gaze.

"Jesus H. Christ! I'm sorry. I didn't hear you come in, um…" Fiona struggled to make out the name on his uniform.

"Trooper LaCroix. Gabriel. Gabe, preferably."

"Let me help you remember. My name is Gabriel. Gabe, preferably." She swallowed hard, her dream dropping piece by piece into her brain. "I hope I didn't keep you waiting too long, Gabe." Her heart skipped.

Gabe's golden-brown irises met hers. "It's no problem. I've always enjoyed watching an intelligent woman read. Fiona, right? You pout in the prettiest way when you do."

Her lips managed half a smile. "Thank you."

He only nodded in response, his look holding hers.

"The usual then?" Fiona turned, trying to hide her mix of anxiety and confusion. "Hazelnut macchiato with grass-fed cow's milk on its way." She could feel his eyes on her back.

"You know I like it natural."

She handed him the cup, half of her wanting to run. "There ya go, Gabe."

"Thanks. Talk to you soon, Fiona."

As soon as his uniformed back was out of sight, she ran into the bathroom. Up came her lunch, then the breakfast before it. Life had gotten way too weird for her stomach to handle.

ॐ

Fiona listened to the waves break around her. *A canopy bed on a tropical beach. What could be better than this?*

Gabe's uniformed figure slid onto bed next to her. He said nothing but kissed her neck and moved down to her breasts. She sighed as his tongue slid around one hard nipple and his fingers played gently with the other. Her hips bucked towards him, the fabric of his uniform teasing her nude skin. "Gabe."

Her hands moved to the buttons of his uniform, fumbling and tearing at them. She slid her hand into the shirt and pressed it against his chest, feeling the steady *thump-thump* of his heart. She brought her eyes to his. "I missed you, Gabe."

7

He laughed deep in his throat. "Now you're remembering." Working his way down her stomach, he tenderly nipped the delicate skin one moment, then kissed it the next. He stopped right before the coarse, red trail leading to her womanhood and nuzzled the spot with the tip of his nose. "I like that you've left some proof."

"I know you like it natural," she breathed, carefully tracing the lines of his widow's peak. Her fingers moved up, teasing the short raven hairs of his crew cut.

Gabe glanced up at her one more time before turning his attention between her thighs. His fingers pressed into her backside, holding her fast to his mouth.

Fiona's back arched as his tongue found the most sensitive spot. "*Fuck*, Gabe." She dug her fingernails into his shoulders, holding him in place until the waves of pleasure ebbed. Her head lulled to the side, and her blue-green eyes closed with a moan.

Gabe moved back up her body. Cool palms cradled her flushed cheeks; Fiona tasted herself on his mouth as he kissed hers. His warm breath tickled as his lips brushed against her ear next. "Please remember soon, Fiona. It's getting bad."

She inhaled deeply, enjoying the smooth scent of sandalwood on him. "I don't understand," came her sleepy reply.

"I know you don't." He exhaled heavily. He kissed her forehead before he left.

Fiona opened her heavy eyelids to find herself in her own bedroom. The best parts of her dream came back as she hugged herself. *Gabe in that uniform. His fragrance. This infatuation.*

Her fingers took on a life of their own as they moved over her body.

Two

Fiona ran.

It wasn't that she particularly enjoyed the activity nor was it the way she wanted to spend her day off. *This is self-flagellation. You deserve this,* she lectured as her sneakers pounded the trail. Her face burned as she recalled waking up in sheets reeking of pleasure and soaked with sweat. *You've got to stop thinking of that man.*

Running in the park didn't prove to be such a horrible reprimand, however; she found it soothing despite herself. Bright green leaves had begun to cover the naked limbs of maples, oaks, and birches. Brilliant yellow daffodils and a rainbow of pansies bloomed in the warm West Virginia spring. Children's laughter echoed from a far-off swing set. Gabe's tall frame held downward dog among a group doing yoga in the park.

Fiona tripped, yelping, "Fuck!"

The yogis turned as one. Gabe popped out of the pose and trotted over to her. "Fiona." He knelt next to her. "Are you okay?"

Gabe laid a hand on her shoulder as she pulled herself up. "Yeah. I—" She cradled her head as a shooting pain ran behind her eyes. "Mebbe not." The world narrowed to a pinpoint as she fell forward into his arms.

࿐

Fiona tugged at the chain holding her to the stone wall, then glanced at Gabriel; the antler tattoos running up his arms and chest glistened with sweat in the flickering torchlight. He nodded, making the chain attached to his collar rattle. As one, their heads moved in the direction of the robed men in front of them. Fiona growled and lunged forward, hitting one priest with a left hook that knocked him to the ground. She bared her pearly teeth, victorious.

Gabe's laugh shook him. "You cannot tame us, idiots. We are not here to do your bidding." The guttural language made his usually smoky voice ominous. He spat, hitting another priest in the face.

The priest kicked Gabriel hard enough to halt the laughter and take his breath away. The captive coughed and spat a gob of blood on the damp stone floor.

Fiona knelt next to her consort and petted his dark, cropped hair. "We are not here to do your bidding. You do not know what you ask," she growled, glancing up at her captors.

"We know exactly what we ask," came a gruff voice from under a hood. "We called upon you. You are ours. You will destroy our enemy."

The captives heads turned toward one another slowly, but the priests didn't understand their smiles.

"We *were* fierce, weren't we?"

Another Fiona, engrossed in the scene, sighed. "You do enjoy invading my dreams, don't you?" She studied the pair in front of her; they were nude, feral-eyed, and filthy and radiated an ancient aura despite their youthful faces. Her pink lips pursed as she turned her gaze on modern-day Gabe.

"No, but it's the only way to help you remember. If I said the things to you in the waking world, you would think I'm crazy." His eyes moved to the collared pair. "This isn't a dream, though." He took her hand. "This is a memory."

"You will destroy our enemies, slaves!"

Fiona took in the scene. One robed man swung a censer on a chain, spreading sickeningly sweet smoke throughout the cell. The others formed a half circle around the pair and began chanting in the harsh language.

"They had no idea what we are," Fiona stated.

Gabe grinned. "They hadn't a clue."

The Fiona of memory tilted her head. "Destroy their enemies, they ask." A finger moved down between her consort's pectoral muscles. "What say you, lover?"

Gabriel traced his tongue along the green vines and vermillion roses tattooed on Fiona's shoulders and chest. "I say we give them what they want. We are *their* slaves." His hands lifted her by the hips and guided her down onto his manhood. He bit his lip, moaning, as his lover slid up and down slowly. "Tell them," he ordered, ruddy light glimmering in his tawny eyes.

Fiona reached out and yanked the closest cleric toward her. She held the stunned man's ear close to her lips and licked his earlobe. "We don't just destroy your enemies. We destroy this entire world," the redhead whispered breathlessly before throwing him against the stone.

The man sat stunned as realization dawned on him. "Stop! Stop them!" He frantically crawled toward them. A shaking hand grabbed at Fiona; she backhanded him with all her might, sending him reeling.

The chanting ceased as his fellow priests stared at him.

"Pull them apart! They'll kill us all!" His hood fell as he struggled to his feet. Firelight flickered in his frenzied eyes as they turned toward the copulating pair.

The clerics moved, but it was too late. Fiona's vine-covered back arched, and Gabe dug his fingers into her hips. A flash of blood-red light filled the room as they orgasmed in unison.

Fiona jumped. "I forgot how intense it is!"

Gabe released an amused *hmm* and squeezed her thigh. "You've forgotten a lot, but it seems to be coming back. Try hard to remember." He rose and walked from her.

"Wait! Where are you going?"

He turned. "Wake up and we'll talk."

�∞�

Fiona growled in the back of her throat as she awoke, the dream fading as she rubbed her eyes. She stretched her arms high above her head before rising to water the String-of-pearls and Dicondra Silver Falls plants that hung in front of the bedroom windows.

She next pulled her long, thick hair into a messy bun, then threw on her favorite pair of cotton panties and cami. A purr left her as she gave herself the once over in her vanity mirror. Her eyes ran over the moss-green vines and vermillion roses decorating her shoulders and chest.

Why do I feel like I'm forgetting something?

She shrugged the feeling off. "Let Operation Day-Off-Comfy-Fi begin."

Comfort? How's that song go? Something about comfort being a mystery... The lyrics always seem to invade her mind when she least expected them. *Damn you, Maynard James Keenan.*

She pouted and stepped into the hallway. Her brain never forgot her true feelings toward life, but she couldn't say she enjoyed the reminders it tossed at her.

Her bare feet automatically lead to the coffee pot, which she found empty. "I know I set this last night. What the he—

"Fuck," she whispered, noticing an oddly comfortable-looking Gabe napping on her tan suede couch. Her morning run came back like a boomerang to the face.

Fiona tried her damnedest not to overtly stare at him in the Purple Bear, so, after quietly starting a pot of coffee, she turned to study him as he slept. One well-muscled arm draped over his head, blocking the sun coming through the living room window; she could see the black ink of a tattoo peek from his sleeve but couldn't quite make the design out. *Maybe tribal?* Her eyes moved to his face, trying to figure out his ethnicity, but his features seemed strangely exotic in places: an alluring mix of Italian, Native American, and something she couldn't quite come up with. *Polish? French? Oh well, easy to look at in any case.* She scanned down the six-foot-three body and bit her lip, trying unsuccessfully not to think about the night's dream. "Mmm. You are gorgeous, Gabriel LaCroix."

"How're you feeling, Fiona?"

The smoky voice jolted Fiona from her reverie. "I was fine until the heart attack you just gave me." He snorted in amusement, pulling himself upright. "Thank you for helping me home—" a tinge of embarrassment gave her pause before saying his name "—Gabe."

Gabe shrugged, his amber eyes meeting hers with an unspoken question.

The unsaid query tugged at Fiona's brain. *What the hell else does he expect me to say? Those eyes of his—the color of a hawk's.* She chewed on the inside of her cheek and turned toward the coffee pot. "Coffee," she stated more than asked, pouring it into two mugs. "It's not your usual, but I do have—"

"Fiona?"

A sharp exhalation left her as she set the carafe down. "I get the feeling you expect something of me, but I don't, for the life of me, know what that would be." A newspaper headline grabbed her attention as she turned back to him: "35 Dead in Suicide Bombing." A lock of bright red-brown hair fell over an eye as she shook her head. "This world…" she mumbled.

Undeniable mischief flashed across his handsome face. "Do you not remember our, um, nocturnal meetings?"

Blood burned her cheeks as her eyes moved to the floor.

"Ah, I thought so. I knew you'd remember the dreams, especially last night's. Let me guess, you were running to punish yourself. You always enjoy a little flagellation—" he moved to the refrigerator and pulled out a bottle of cream "—though self-flagellation in the form of cardio is new." He poured some into both mugs and moved back to the couch with his.

Fiona remained frozen a moment, then threw the newspaper at him, half hoping to inflict a vicious paper cut. "You talk as if you've known me forever." She paused as another headline caught her attention: "Student Admits to Frat Rape Lie." "What the hell is wrong with people?" she breathed with an uncomfortable shiver.

He mumbled something she couldn't make out, folded the newspaper, and placed it on the coffee table.

Fiona grabbed her mug and sat on the other end of the couch. "Well, enigmatic statements are wonderful, but how'd you get into my apartment? More importantly, how do you know where I live?" Before he could answer, she shot "Most importantly—now that I think about it— should you have let me go to sleep with a head injury?" at him.

Gabe sipped his coffee. "Your key and ID were in that little hidden pocket they put in gym shorts, but, being a cop, I can find out someone's address if I have to. You didn't hit your head, though." He set the mug on a coaster. "But your hands and knees are a little worse for wear… And I have known you forever."

A frustrated groan drowned out his last statement as she noticed the fresh red scrapes on her palms. "Wait, no. I must have hit my head, too. I blacked out."

Uncomfortable embarrassment spread over Gabe's features. "You passed out when I touched your shoulder."

Great, Fi! All those years living rough and this is the time you weren't vigilant. Good job! Her brain scrambled for a logical answer as her eyes narrowed in suspicion. "Did-did you slip me something? Honestly, I have been in worse situations and I'm—"

"What?" She noticed hurt in his eyes as he cut her off. "*No.* Fuck no." He threw his hands up, then quickly calmed himself. "It must have been, well, I think, it was my touch. Then we shared a memory." He looked at her expectantly.

She met the amber orbs as parts of her dream returned: saccharine sweet smoke, chanting priests, wild-eyed versions of herself and Gabe chained to a wall. *"This isn't a dream, though. It's a memory."*

"Mmm, a dungeon? Creepy clerics? You and me chained to a wall? The world going red?"

Coffee spilled over the rim of the mug as her heart lurched. She quickly set it down, her hands trembling.

"You do then." He took a long drink. "I should've known this would take some time. You threatened to forget so many times."

Fiona pinched the bridge of her nose and shook her head slowly from side to side. "Forget? What exactly do I need to remember?"

"Who you are. What we have to do." He sighed. "It's time. We can't deny it."

"And who am I?" *"Mother Convicted in Infant Drowning Death." Christ sakes,* she thought. *Why am I noticing all the worst headlines today?* "Besides the best barista in Randolph County, West By-God Virginia?"

Gabe tilted his head and lifted an eyebrow with a half-smile. "We created this world, and now we have to destroy it."

Her eyebrows raised as she guffawed. "How exactly did you get into the police, Gabriel LaCroix, with you being bat-shit insane and all?" She stood up and walked back to the counter.

"If you think I'm crazy," he started softly, "then why aren't you frightened? For the most part, I'm a stranger, but you poured me coffee and sat down next to me as if I'm an old friend. You must remember something— maybe deep down—or you wouldn't be so comfortable being half-clothed in front of me." He paused seeming to chew over something. "Especially with things that have happened in your past."

She stomped over in front of him, then crossed her arms over her breasts, suddenly aware of her lack of coverage. "What exactly would you know of it?" Her adopted brother's lecherous grin flashed across her mind, causing a shudder of revulsion to pass through her.

Gabe rested his elbows on his thighs and rubbed his face in his hands. "You had to make this difficult. Damn it," he grumbled, flexing his long fingers. "I have a feeling I'm going to *royally* screw this up, but you *know* there's something different about you. You've know for a very long time. You've never felt like you've fit into this world. I know. Others feel it, too. The way people look at you sometimes. The odd expressions. Not everyone, obviously, but Justin felt it. What he did—" He ducked as Fiona threw a left hook; she stared at him in surprise. "That's the first time you ever missed with one of those. I remembered for once."

She slapped the self-satisfied expression from his face with the other hand, wobbling as a stab of pain blurred her vision. Suddenly sensitive to the sunlight brightening the room, she snapped her eyelids down. "Don't you dare vindicate that bastard. Good reason to rape me. I'm fucking *special,*" she spat, opening her eyes.

Gabe moved his jaw back and forth, recovering from the blow. "I'm not justifying it—*fuck that hurt*—he—"

"Please leave now, Gabe." Fiona tried in vain to avoid his amber irises.

The man drained his coffee and stood up. "I went about this completely wrong, but I never claimed to be the smart one here. Things are coming back to you." He glanced at the newspaper as he walked past her. "You're noticing things you never noticed before." She heard him pause at the table by the door and scratch something on the pad of paper there. "You'll want to know more soon." The door opened and closed quietly as he left.

Fiona curled herself into a ball on the couch, her head throbbing with her pulse. Memories of her brother and parents reared as she squeezed her eyes shut. "Dammit. Crazy bastard. Special." She inhaled deeply, trying to quell the migraine, and cursed at the pleasant, earthy musk filling her nostrils. "Of course you would smell like Gabe now, couch. Thanks for nothing."

Three

Fiona breathed in the salty air and took a step into the warm waves before the note sprang into her brain.

Turn around tonight, Fiona.

She never thought to look behind her in the world between waking life and dreams. The hazy timberline of a forest met her gaze as she glanced over her shoulder. Her feet lead slowly from the ocean and crossed the sand.

☙❧

Fiona's jaw dropped as she stared up at the primeval forest surrounding her. Massive oaks stretched hundreds of feet into the clear, blue sky, nearly blocking out the sun. Rogue beams of light came in through leaf-covered limbs, illuminating the dewy moss clinging to the bases of trees and rocks. Dead leaves crunched under her bare feet as she carefully padded along. A stream babbled cheerfully nearby.

"Home," she sighed, inhaling the scent of decaying leaves and soil. Her eyes closed halfway before she roughly shook her head. "Why would I think that?"

A cry from afar made her scramble behind a tree before she had time to think more on it. She peeked around the trunk as the sound of feet pounding the path grew closer.

Another Fiona turned her head to keep tabs on her pursuer. She screamed again and hurried on, panting.

Fiona studied her counterpart with curiosity, feeling as though she were critiquing a portrait. A sheen of perspiration made the oval face glitter in the stray beams of sunlight. She could finally see why people referred to her as elfin: petite stature, large eyes, delicate straight nose, pouty cupid lips. Vine and rose tattoos decorated the alabaster chest, back, and shoulders just like they did hers. Long Titian hair fell past her buttocks in braids and loose waves.

"Not fear," the present-day woman realized, gazing into the cerulean eyes. "Excitement…"

A heartbeat later, Gabriel, clad in antlers and leather breeches, came running up the path. He tackled his prey; they rolled together through the leaves until he pinned her to the ground. Fiona fought and bucked, managing to turn the tables in her favor. She clambered away, but Gabe grabbed her ankle and dragged her towards him. He crawled on top of her and ran a hand up her naked thigh. She shrieked, clawing at the ground in front of her.

Blood burned in modern-day Fiona's cheeks. *Rape?* She shuddered violently. *Wait... No... Foreplay? You always enjoy a little flagellation,* her mind joked, mocking Gabe's voice. *Keep watching. Remember this.*

Ancient Fiona struggled against Gabe and turned over. Her fingertips traced the antlers tattooed on his upper arms, shoulders, and chest, then her nails dug into his heaving chest. His head went back with a groan as she grinned. Their eyes met as her hands moved down his body.

Gabe ripped Fiona's deer skin vest loose, biting his lip as he gazed down at her bare breasts. She grabbed the antlers and pulled his head down, arching herself toward him as his teeth gently grazed her nipple. His hand moved down her slender stomach and untied her skirt, then he slid his fingers into her. Fiona let go of his antlers and dug her fingernails into the dead leaves surrounding her, her body surrendering to his touch. He cocked his head to the side, watching her pleasure with hungry eyes.

Fiona recovered her composure and rolled Gabe onto his back, straddling him. She pinned his arms to his sides and ran her tongue over the black lines of his tattoo. His tawny eyes rolled back as his head lolled to the side, a deep moan parting his full lips. Fiona released his wrists and clutched the antlers once more. Turning his head towards her, she slid her tongue between his lips and moved her hips side to side slowly. Her fingers moved down through his cropped raven hair, then one traced a line from the tip of his widow's peak down to his mouth. She nipped his bottom lip playfully, then let the tip of her tongue work down his glistening body.

Fiona craned her neck for a closer view as her primeval self untied Gabriel's buck skin breeches and exposed him. "Oh," she murmured, delighting in the perfection and size of his manhood before it disappeared into her twin's mouth. She quickly looked around her, expecting modern Gabe laughing at her, but she was thankfully still alone.

Gabe's fingers laced themselves into the Titian waves of ancient Fiona's hair and tugged as her head glided up and down. After a few minutes, he pulled her back up to his face and hungrily brought her mouth to his.

Fiona cried out as Gabe rolled her once again onto her stomach. Fingers dug into the creamy flesh of her hips and pulled her onto all fours. He tenderly slid himself into her body with a low moan; Fiona arched her back and pressed her backside against him.

Fiona found herself watching with voyeuristic excitement. Their bodies flowed together as smoothly as water over the stones in the stream behind her. A rosy flush moved up other Fiona's chest as Gabriel moved faster and harder against her. Their skin shimmered ethereally as the noises escaping them became more animalistic: groans and grunts of contentment mixed with the longing ache that comes as one approaches the crest.

"Shit." Modern Fiona cowered behind the tree as she remembered the scarlet flash of her last memory.

A burst of white and a rush of heat knocked her off her feet instead. She lay on her back, panting. "It's still here," she whispered, breathing in the smell of wet leaves.

She pulled herself to her feet and peeked around the tree trunk. Gabe lay propped up on a fallen tree, cradling his lover against him. His fingers twirled locks of red hair around themselves. Fiona nuzzled his bare chest, tracing the lines of his muscles and tattoo. He tilted her chin up and kissed the tip of her nose.

"I need to talk to Gabe. I need to remember who I am," she said to herself just before the alarm jerked her awake.

Four

"Fi? Fi-ooo-na?" Jaime waved a hand in front of the barista's face.

She snapped from her reverie. "Huh?"

"You've been staring at the door for, like, an hour now. Are you expecting Publisher's Clearing House to walk in?"

"I'm waiting for Gabe," she answered absentmindedly, turning back to the glass door to survey the sidewalk.

"Gabe? Who's—" Her boss inhaled and covered his mouth as he let out an eager squeak. "Is *that* Hot Cop's name? Oooohh. We're on a first name basis with him now. You *do* realize it's in your contract to give me *all* the details, should you two hook up?"

Fiona turned toward him and lifted her eyebrows in amusement. "I somehow do not recall reading that bit, Mister Hess."

"Oh, the, um, Sexy Partner Clause. It was there. Or maybe it was just implied. Throw me a fucking bone, Fi! There aren't all that many gorgeous guys in this god-forsaken hole we call Laurel Springs!"

"I promise—if it happens—I'll give you details." She smiled softly at him. "I don't know if it'll come to all that. He helped me out the other day, but I haven't seen him since. I'm starting to worry something bad happened to him—him being a cop and this world the way it is."

Jaime cocked his blond head. "You've decided to start paying attention to the news then? Wow. Here I thought you enjoyed ignorance. This world's been pure shit for quite a while now."

Fiona wished she could stop paying attention, but the news stalked her now. Reports of disgusting crimes assaulted her ears no matter what radio station or television channel she tuned to. Vile headlines jumped into her view, bringing bile to her throat: mothers murdering their children; men forcing themselves on women; humans torturing animals; groups violently imposing their ideals on others; so-called holy men condemning innocents; government choosing profits over the best interest of their people; people overdosing their lives away. She'd never been one to enjoy television, but some twisted compulsion forced her to turn her tiny set on now; Gabe's visit cursed her with curiosity and clarity, even with her supposed truant memory.

"I think you're going through 'Hot Cop Withdrawal,'" Jaime stated bumping her shoulder playfully. "Not seeing that beautiful ass of his could give anyone the DTs, really.

My prescription would be to watch some reruns of *COPS* or *Alaska State Troopers*. They both have some hotties."

She whacked him with a newspaper.

Withdrawal was a real factor and not just because of his attractiveness. He'd been AWOL for nearly a week. No further memories revealed themselves during slumber. Dreams were Gabe-free. He avoided the shop. She figured he was giving her space and time after the way they'd left it, but she needed to talk to him.

"Oh! Assault! Assault!" Jaime cried, making his husky voice effeminate. "I'm gonna call the police!"

Fiona shook her head as they both fell into a fit of giggles, annoying a group snapping photos of her foam art for Instagram.

࿇

Fiona's heart drummed double time as her eyes moved from the paper in her hand to the door in front of her. *55 Bent Maple Road, Apt. F* written neatly in Gabe's handwriting stared back at her. Going to him was her last resort.

After a few deep breaths, she rapped her knuckles on the door. Her eyes closed as the sound of footsteps grew louder. "Not ready for this. Not ready," she whispered as she heard locks unlatching.

A uniform-clad Gabe greeted her. "Fiona. Hi."

29

Her heart skipped, both relieved he was okay and terrified at being at his home. "Oh, I'm sorry. You're on your way to work." She turned on her heels.

"I just got home," he replied. "Come in."

Fiona swallowed hard as she silently turned and followed him into the apartment, gently closing the door behind her.

"How've you been?" he asked, tugging his shirt from his trousers.

"I've been better in this life."

Gabe nodded slowly, giving her a knowing gaze. "Make yourself comfortable. I'm going to change." He walked into his bedroom.

Fiona stood a minute, fidgeting with a ring around her finger, then trailed behind him. She leaned silently against the doorframe and watched him unbutton the forest-green shirt, shrug it off, and hang it up with military care. "What's all that?"

Gabe glanced over his shoulder in surprise, then looked down at the black vest covering his chest. "Kevlar. Body armor."

Fiona moved closer to study it as he began unstrapping the vest; she ran her fingers over it and wrinkled her nose. "It doesn't seem like much."

"It does its job, trust me. The world's a dangerous place and some people love the thought of dead cop," he added, watching her.

She agreed with a grunt. "I've been noticing how dangerous lately." Realizing how close she was to him, she stepped back uncomfortably. "It's like you fucking cursed me." She sat on his bed and stared at the rug beside it.

Gabe knelt on one knee in front of her as she lifted her chin. "It was only a matter of time, Fiona. I'm sorry." He stood back up, finished unstrapping the Kevlar vest, laying it carefully on a chair, then unhooked his belt and hung up his uniform pants.

"That's gotta be a bitch in this heat," she remarked, observing the sweat staining his white T-shirt.

"You get used to it. Plus, it's the only thing between me and a bullet." He pulled the damp shirt over his head and tossed it in a hamper.

Fiona admired the way his back tapered into a muscular V before he turned to find a clean shirt. The antler tattoo decorating his chest and arms drew her eye next. *Just like the memory.*

He pulled on a pair of khaki shorts and moss-green T-shirt. "I'm guessing you came here for a reason. Let's talk."

❧

Gabe got up and grabbed two more beers as Fiona finished telling him the memory. He handed her the full bottle of IPA, deftly avoiding her bare skin, then made himself comfortable once again on the other end of the couch.

She took a long drink, thinking for a moment. "It took me a while to figure out after the memory, but, at my apartment, you told me we created this world and we now have to destroy it." He nodded. "But…I still don't understand who or what this makes me. *Us*."

He mulled over her statement. "The best guess we've ever had to what we are is primordial spirits." She lifted a questioning eyebrow at him. "Hey, don't give me that look, it's mostly *your* theory. We never really thought twice about our existence until those freak clerics figured out how to pull us from the Forest. I liked to think god and goddess, but you said that sounded conceited. Before that, our lives were simple: hunting, screwing, playing, more screwing." He grinned devilishly as he took a swig from his bottle. "Apparently we bore a few different worlds in the process."

"The white flash?" She recalled how their bodies shimmered as they grew closer to climax and the pure heat of the burst of light.

"Yes, when we really got worked up, like in that memory."

Fiona's lips formed a wry smile. "That must be some fantastic sex."

"Oh, yes," he breathed with a cocksure grin, "it is." They both laughed. "I'm not sure how many worlds we created, but those clerics brought us to this world." His smile faded. "I still don't know exactly what they thought they'd bring themselves, but we were not what they were after."

"We annihilated their world in that memory we shared."

"We destroyed a version of their world—*this world*." Gabe's golden eyes shifted up to the right as he thought, an endearing habit Fiona noticed he possessed. "After a week in chains, you figured out what they wanted: us to annihilate their enemy. You knew it wouldn't be as selective as they desired. You cannot kill that which you did not create, you said. We conceived this universe and however many more. Duty dictated we destroy it when necessary. All of it." A noisy rush of air left his throat. "That was only the first time. Those priests created some kind of unbreakable link between us and this world. Every time humanity turns to shit, this universe cries out and we're pulled from the comfort of our wood to fix things."

"The scarlet destruction."

A corner of his full lips turned up. "I know you don't remember, but you named it that after the first time."

"It's fitting," she replied, finishing the last of her beer. The talk deserved more of a hard liquor in her opinion, but she retrieved another two from the fridge regardless. She set one down in front of him.

"That it is. I've always felt we cauterize the wounds of this world." He popped the tops from the bottles.

Fiona gazed around Gabe's living room as she let the information sink in. The place had a just-moved-in feel: only a few pieces of furniture and a smattering of posters and pictures on the walls.

An awkward silence blanketed the room. She turned her head and studied him. "All the people?"

His eyes met hers. "They go with it. Though, it seems, they're born with some kind of innate memory. They always seem to have some kind of creation myth involving us. Kinda like Adam and Eve."

"No, I mean, do they feel the pain? Do they suffer?"

She thought of Jaime, her sole friend, and their first encounter.

"Living on the streets?" the husky voice asked when she walked into the Purple Bear. She barely inclined her head in response, waiting for him to throw her out. "Know anything about coffee?"

"More than a little and less than everything."

An odd look shot her way. "I'll fill you in. You're hired."

"I...I don't believe so. I imagine, for all of them, it's like being at ground zero when a bomb goes off. There one minute...then nothing." His eyes moved from hers. "This is the first time you've ever wondered that, you know."

Fiona closed her eyes. "Show me another memory." Pain flashed across her eyelids as Gabe's fingers laced into hers.

Five

Greasy smoke filled the tower room with the scent of roasting rabbit.

The smell roused Fiona into consciousness. She found herself in the crook of Gabe's arm; he ran a reassuring hand down her back as she sat up. "This is the last time we annihilated this world. It was simpler then, and we were *very* different than we are now." They turned their attention to the scene before them.

Heavy chains clanked as Gabriel of memory awoke.

"Don't fret now, I'm here." Long Titian braids bobbed around her shoulders as Fiona turned to him with a smirk. Splatters of blood stained her doeskin jerkin, britches, and thigh-high leather boots. A dagger hung at her hip.

"What're you doing?" her captive asked hoarsely.

"Counting bodies." She turned back to the small window to face a sky orange from reflected fires. "Sometimes they fall just as the war drums pound." Cerulean eyes coldly surveyed the scene below.

Gabriel tried to reach the window, but the chains tripped him.

"Step away from the window. Your love of this world disgusts me. Go back to sleep until you're ready."

He pulled himself up and reached out to grab her, but she sidestepped in time to elude him. He beat his fists on the stone wall. "Fiona! This is madness! Let me go!"

She ignored his cries in favor of turning the cooking rabbit.

He sat with a frustrated huff.

Present day Fiona turned to Gabe. "Did you not want to fix this world?"

Gabe silently led her to the window and studied the scene below, but she stared quietly at her ancient self. *How could that be me?* The delicate features she admired in the forest seemed alien now. A jaded scowl marred the contented countenance she had previously seen. Anger and frustration burned in her striking blue orbs.

When she finally let her eyes follow her guide's gaze, vomit rose in her throat. She clamped a hand clamped over her mouth.

The ruins of a few keeps and a handful of stout trees dotted the scorched earth below. Blood pooled like ponds as filthy warriors opened the throats of screaming children. Fire pits dotted the landscape; a group of chain-mail clad women led a downtrodden group of prisoners to one and pushed them in, drinking in their anguished screams with satisfaction.

"Are those screams animal or human?" Gabriel questioned.

A smoky haze wafted into the room, waging battle with the cooking smells.

Fiona returned to the window as the war drums pounded faster. "You know them to be human. They've begun burning people alive." She glared at him. "*We have to end this, Gabriel.*"

His lip rose as he snarled at her, then he cackled maniacally. "No, Fiona. You have to let me go."

Gabe studied his former self with narrowed eyes. "I didn't want to fix this world." He cast his eyes down. "I joined the people on the killing fields. I enjoyed it. That was where you found me. You knocked me out with the broadside of your sword and dragged me up here." He pinched the bridge of his nose. "Please say something. Anything."

Shame showed on his handsome face. Fiona squeezed his hand in an attempt to soothe him. "What were they fighting over?" She motioned to the group below.

"Religion. Seems to be recurring with the denizens of this universe. If it's not religion, it's usually race. They can be sadly predictable."

Ancient Fiona snapped around and leapt on the chained man, pinning his arms to the rough stone floor. "We are going to do this. This fucking world called to us, fucking screamed in fucking pain." She snatched the dagger from her side and deftly sliced through the laces of his pants.

Gabriel took advantage of his newly freed hand and wrapped it around Fiona's slender throat. Strangled cries escaped her as the blade slipped from her fingers. She clawed at his face. He sneered as blood ran down his cheek. "I *will* get out of these chains, cunt."

"*Holy shit.*" Watching yourself being strangled hardly seemed like a luxury, but Fiona watched with horrified curiosity as her ancient self struggled and fought, face turning red, then purple. She noticed Gabe shift uncomfortably as he stared at the floor.

The leather-clad Fiona's limbs fell limp at her sides as she ceased fighting. The captive loosened his grip and let her body fall into his arms, his lips trembling a brief moment as he gazed down. He placed her more gently than his tiny audience expected on the cold stone floor, touching her pale face, then kissed her dirty forehead before beginning his search for the shackle keys.

"Is she—am *I* dead?"

A left hook knocking Gabriel against the wall answered the question. He sputtered as she stood. "When have I ever been easy to kill?" She aimed a round of hard kicks into his gut. "Eyes up here. *Watch.*" He groaned in agony as she pulled the key from between her breasts and walked to the window. "There goes any chance you had," she chided, tossing the key into the wasteland.

His howl joined those of the people below.

Fiona strode over to him and lifted him by his vest to his feet. She tore it open, studied the musculature a brief moment, then ran her tongue over the lines of the antlers.

Modern Fiona took in the scene with her head tilted. "We always have our tattoos."

Gabe nodded, seeming relieved as the focus shifted from their former selves. "They're part of us. The flora and the fauna. We came into every incarnation, except our present, close to what's considered adulthood, tattoos included. I still don't know what happened this time around." He gazed at her. "Did you not feel empty before you got it in this life?" He touched the pattern decorating her collarbone.

"On the streets at sixteen leaves a lot to be desired, Gabe LaCroix," she mumbled. She closed her eyes and sighed, recalling the burning pain of the needle as it colored her skin. The feeling of wholesomeness warmed her once again as she remembered studying the raw skin in the tattoo parlor's mirror. "I did feel...incomplete before it."

Ancient Gabriel pushed Fiona away, but she came back, squeezing his face in her hands. He head butted her, splitting her bottom lip. She licked the blood with ecstasy, then forced her mouth on his. Gabriel pushed her to the floor, but she gained the upper hand before he could restrain her. Her nails raked over the bare skin of his stomach as he bucked, digging his dirty fingers into her hip bones. Fiona released a cry of mingled pain and passion as Gabriel threw her to the floor. He held her head back by a handful of tangled red hair and ripped her jerkin open. She bit her lip as his mouth found her breasts.

"Mmmm. That's more like it, Gabriel. I knew a row would get you going." Her hand slid into the crotch of his britches, pulling out his manhood. She shimmied her own pants down and slid him inside with a delighted moan.

They matched the frenzied rhythm of the war drums. The red flash came quickly.

Fiona's eyes searched the nothingness around her. "Cauterized the wound."

"Yes." Gabe smirked. "We weren't at our best, but we did what we had to." He intently studied his flexing fingers.

"What would have happened if you had killed me?" Fiona asked, breaking the tense silence that had fallen.

Just as Gabe's lips parted to answer, the ringing of a phone jolted them from the memory. Fiona inhaled sharply and clutched the sofa cushions, her entire body shaking. Gabe groped for his cell phone.

She watched his smooth brow furrow as he listened to the caller. "I'll be there soon." He turned to her, concern clouding his eyes. "I've got to go to work. Something's happened. I'll drive you home."

Six

Fiona unchained the door, letting the worried-looking state trooper into her apartment. "My neighbors are going to think I'm in trouble. First, you drop me off in a cruiser, then you show up in uniform. Go all blues-and-twos, and I don't know what they'll think."

He snorted in amusement before carefully setting his cap down and sitting on the sofa.

"What's going on?" She re-chained the door before plopping down on the sofa just far enough away not to touch him. Physical contact opened the door to memory; she wanted to learn news of the present.

Gabe stared at her with his raven eyebrows raised. "You haven't been watching the news? Honestly?"

"No," she answered avoiding his eyes. "I-I've been trying to remember more. By myself." His face quickly changed from annoyed to apologetic to hopeful. "No dice. I still feel like the lowly barista Fiona Albright. Despite all you've shown me, I don't feel like the mother—or destroyer, for that matter—of universes, unfortunately."

The corners of her mouth turned down briefly before she decided to change the subject. "So…what kind of shit is going on now?"

He leaned forward and rested his elbows on his uniformed thighs, lacing his fingers together. "Remember that man who got shot by a sheriff's deputy a few weeks back? In the West Side?"

The West Side of Laurel Springs, West Virginia, possessed few redeeming qualities to most residents. Businesses barred their store fronts because of crime. Apartment buildings and homes there were blamed for lowered property values in the rest of the city. Belle Boyd College warned their coeds to avoid the area. Dealing meth and heroin were the biggest businesses in that part of town.

Fiona had avoided numerous areas like the West Side during her two years living on the streets and, thankfully, never needed anything provided there.

Though when the shooting happened Fiona ignored the news, she paid attention no matter what now. Half the town raged, calling it murder, while the other half defended the officer. Many were calling it mistreatment of minorities, since the man who died had been black. The deceased's family, among others, called for justice: The deputy needed to be prosecuted and imprisoned. Still others feared a race riot was building. People in other cities across the country staged sympathetic protests. The sleepy college town of fifteen thousand shook.

Fiona studied it everyday in the papers. The stories always conflicted: the deceased, a mere man-child, was murdered in cold-blood by a racist deputy versus the deputy defended himself accordingly against a violent offender.

She failed to make a judgment either way. Growing up, she'd found herself in bad situations and defended herself the way she felt necessary. At the same time, she felt for both the deceased's family for losing a child and for the officer who had to make the decision to take a life in order to protect his own.

"The Grand Jury didn't indict the deputy."

While Fiona's sigh indicated relief, Gabe's did not. Realization dawned on her. "Fuck." She tilted her head back and stared up at the ceiling.

"They want blood, Fiona. What they consider justice." He turned to her. "After the announcement, the father called for the city to burn." An amused *huh* escaped his throat. "They hate cops, yet I have to be out there."

Her head snapped around. "No. You have to stay safe." She pursed her lips and turned her eyes away awkwardly.

Gabe rubbed his face in his hands. "I'm glad to know you're worried, even if you can't remember who I am to you." He exhaled heavily and tried to play off his own worry. "I'll be in riot gear, heavily armed."

Fiona found the fear hiding in the amber irises as his usual confidence cracked ever so slightly.

Gabe gazed down at his hands, flexing his fingers and turning up his palms to calm his nerves. "You asked me what would happen if I had killed you in the last memory we shared." She nodded. "This is not the first time we've been called to this version of this universe. It's been a hazardous place. World War One. World War Two. It screamed to us both times, but we failed it. Ready?"

Instead of wrapping his fingers around hers, he wrapped an arm around her back and caressed her bare shoulder. His daring coupled with the intimacy of the gesture caught her breath in her throat just before she felt herself fall gently against his chest.

❧❧

"You're getting more accustomed to my touch." Gabe stared into the haze of the in-between world.

"Mmm. Not painful this time. A soft fog descending on my brain." Fiona noticed the soft, happy smile on his lips. She glanced around. "Why aren't we in the memory?"

He took her hand. "I carried you to them the last two times. This time we can walk together." Gabe tilted his head down at her. "Don't worry. You're not heavy."

"I get the impression you wouldn't tell me if I were."

The golden eyes moved from her head to her feet, and he wrinkled his nose mischievously. "I can handle five-five, a hundred pounds dripping wet. At least when you're unconscious."

She shoulder-checked him playfully as the haze enveloped them.

༒

Fiona squeezed Gabe's hand and ducked involuntarily as a far-off bomb shook the room.

His fingers squeezed back. "It can't hurt us," he assured her. "Just a memory." He motioned toward a nurse sitting next to a patient, clasping his shaking hand. "The world pulled us here during World War One. Amazes me it took so long."

Fiona studied the scene. A tight bun at the nape of Nurse Fiona's neck kept the ruddy hair neat under a white muslin cap. A clean white apron covered most of the back of the gray serge uniform. A lighter gray band decorated with a red cross wrapped around her left arm. She raised the hand to her mouth and kissed the knuckles. "Gabe."

"Fi," he wheezed in reply, turning her way. "Where am I?"

She brought a glass to his parched lips. "France. Casualty Clearing Station."

47

"We were British," present-day Fiona observed with delight.

"Yes," Gabe answered, enjoying her pleasure.

Another explosion shook them.

"How close were we to the front?" Fiona asked her guide.

"Oh." He puffed up his cheeks. "A few miles behind the front lines. Maybe eight, ten miles away. They kept Casualty Clearing Stations close."

"You finally found me," the other Gabe stated weakly, his breathing rapid. "Though, I think a little too late."

Nurse Fiona mopped his forehead, her lips trembling. "I knew you'd join the army."

He *mmm'd* deep in his throat. "You always like me in uniform."

"You are beautiful in a uniform."

"Don't I know it," both men replied in unison.

Fiona eyed the forest green trooper's uniform. "They do suit you."

Nurse Fiona petted her patient's damp hair. "Gabe—" Her voice cracked.

"I knew you'd follow the fighting. I wish we'd found one another sooner." His hand moved to her face and a thumb wiped away her tears. A shudder wracked his body. "You have to figure out what to do. You're clever. Not like me, getting shot, dying."

"I will," she promised, gazing into his eyes.

"Fi," he sighed as his body relaxed, "the Forest. I can see the Forest."

Her lips parted as his eyelids slid down. "Gabe?" She cradled his pale cheek before placing two fingers on his neck. She choked, then laid her head down on his chest, sobbing.

Modern Gabe let all his breath out at once. "Septicemia. Blood poisoning. I don't recommend it as a way to die."

Nurse Fiona straightened her spine as she sat up, resolve in the damp eyes. Her breasts rose with a few deliberate breaths. She kissed Gabriel's gray lips before standing and scanning the hospital.

She walked calmly to an eerily silent surgery as Gabe and Fiona followed. The nurse paused a moment before approaching a table and picking up a scalpel.

Fiona's hand tightened around Gabe's as her counterpart flicked the blade with her thumb. The nurse unbuttoned her sleeve and balled her fingers into a tight fist, studying the artery. Fiona flinched as she saw the blade move down, but thankfully, the nurse replaced the scalpel with a dismissive shake of her head. She released a long breath. "Gabe?" His eyes shifted to her twin.

Nurse Fiona quietly opened a cabinet, removing a syringe and a few vials. "Morphine. Less mess and so much quicker." She moved back to her lover's corpse and seated herself, placing her lips on his ashen forehead for a silent moment. She deftly stuck the needle into the vial to fill it, then flicked the sharp with a finger. The dim light reflected in her blue-green eyes as she jabbed herself in the crook of her elbow, wincing. In a quick motion, she refilled the syringe and repeated the process.

With a wobbling head, she hid the empty syringe and vials and laced her fingers in her lover's. A long sigh parted her bluish lips as she laid her head down near Gabriel's and placed their hands on his still chest. Labored breaths moved her body as her eyelids drooped. A minute later, she grew still and the haze surrounded her onlookers.

"Are you all right?" Gabe's smoky voice shattered the peacefulness of the In-Between.

Fiona's mouth opened and closed silently as she knitted her brows together. Watching both herself and Gabe die made her stomach cartwheel. She covered her face with her hands to compose herself. "Did I have to do the same in World War Two?"

"No." They walked forward into the ether. "I did."

Seven

The wail of a siren waned to nothing as lights began popping up in the windows of houses. Faces peeked nervously from behind curtains, assessing damage. A few piles of rubble resembled former houses. Fires smoldered in the distance.

"Welcome to London. It's the Blitz."

The blue-gray of a Royal Air Force uniform flashed before them as an airman surveyed the destruction. "Fiona!" Desperation clouded the man's amber eyes. "Fiona!"

"Gabe," came the weak reply.

He darted to the alleyway and skidded to a stop.

Fiona sat propped up against a garden wall, clutching her midsection. Her lips trembled as she studied the scarlet streaks leaking through her fingers, darkening her cobalt blouse.

Sergeant Gabe LaCroix knelt down and cradled her against his chest, placing a hand over hers. He petted her head with the other, leaving the red-gold victory rolls in shambles, and kissed the top of her head. "You'll be fine, Fi. You're not easy to kill. Just hold on." He scooted them against the wall as tears silently ran down his cheeks.

Her eyes moved up to his face as she tried to laugh. "Liar. It went right through me—a pipe or something. I'm dying."

"No, no." Gabe gently rocked back and forth, suppressing sobs. "I just found you, love."

Modern Fiona tilted her head to study the scene, then stared up at her guide. "Are we always separated when we're pulled here?"

Gabe sniffled and wiped his face before meeting her eyes. "We weren't always. Time and again we came here together. We did our duty and found ourselves back home. Seems to me, the worse this universe is, the farther apart we arrive. This incarnation is horrible." He tried to turn before more tears left his eyes.

Fiona wrapped her fingers tighter around his as his sadness washed over her. He returned the squeeze in silent thanks.

"Gabe. Listen to—" A stab of pain shook injured Fiona's lithe frame. "*Fuck.* What is it with these Germans? The Great War, now this horse shi—" She squeezed her eyes closed and inhaled sharply. "If only I could have fought. I could have stayed safe and found you quickly. This universe has never been more shit. Not letting females into battle. I don't underst—" Her teeth gritted together.

The airman chuckled softly through his tears. "They believe you the weaker of the sexes and too distracting to military men. I agree with the second thought. You wielding a broadsword can be very distracting." He nuzzled her temple.

"You know what you have to do." Her pained eyes opened slowly.

He gave a choked sob in reply and buried his face in her hair, nodding. "I know, Fi, I know."

"I'll be waiting." The cerulean irises fixed as her head lolled back against his shoulder.

Gabe rained kisses on her hair, then wept, hugging the limp body to his chest.

Modern Fiona eyed the man beside her from her peripheral. She'd gone her current lifetime without a partner; the loving way airman Gabe held her past self made her regret that decision. *Why would I want to forget this person? Why can't I make myself remember this now?* Light reflected in Gabe's tear-glazed eyes.

Her gaze moved back to the scene as Sergeant LaCroix pulled a revolver from his side. "Enfield number two, thirty-eight," her Gabe mumbled as her heart thudded. The barrel slid between the airman's lips.

"No. Fuck," came out of Fiona as a strangled whisper as he pulled the trigger.

The bullet's force slammed his head against the wall before the body slumped over Fiona's.

Present day Fiona's jaw dropped as she gaped at the gory mix of blood, brains, and bone clinging to the wall as the memory faded.

❧

"I remember dying both times. The searing pain of the blood poisoning the first time. The brief burning in my head the second." His statement was barely audible. "You remember your deaths as well. Well, you did remember."

"Bloody hell," she muttered.

"We end up home, the Forest. The grin on your face when you ran to me…" Gabe shook off the nostalgia. "We didn't get pulled from the Forest immediately in this world's time. Both wars ended with some kind of peace. I dunno. Maybe we forced it to fix itself."

Fiona stared into the whiteness of the haze as she let the deaths she'd watched sink in. "What about this time?"

"We came back as children. The first memory I have is of holding you, a baby, on the porch of a group foster home, 1990. They said I was four; you were one. At first they thought we were brother and sister." He lead her forward. "I won't take you through twenty-five years of details. Just what's important."

❧

A wide-eyed, chipmunk-cheeked boy sat holding a baby with a shock of Titian hair. The girl in moss-green denim overalls smiled up at him as he gazed around in confusion. A tiny hand reached up and tugged at his T-shirt. "Gabe?"

A matronly woman peered down at the pair in concern. "Oh, you poor things," she mumbled before reaching for baby Fiona.

"Miss Jenkins," adult Gabe whispered.

"No!" the boy cried hugging her. The little girl giggled.

Miss Jenkins knelt on one knee to look him in the eyes. "I won't hurt her. Or you. You're safe here. May I have your sister?" He firmly set his jaw and lifted his chin; the woman nodded sadly. "You can carry her in then, son." The raven-haired child stood, making sure the girl was secure, and walked into the house.

The haze segued into another memory.

"You were adorable." Fiona watched as a blush crept up from Gabe's uniform collar.

Young Gabe set down a small suitcase next to Miss Jenkins and baby Fiona, smiling down at the red-haired girl.

"Gabriel?" the woman asked, crouching down. "We talked about this. Fiona is being adopted by the Coopers." The boy gazed up at the couple curiously. The matron turned toward the couple. "Gabriel here was holding Fiona when I found them out front. They're not siblings, but he is quite attached to her." She ran her hand down the curve of the boy's head.

"It's nice to meet you, Gabriel," Mr. Cooper said, offering his hand to the boy. The boy shook it uncomfortably.

Mrs. Cooper crouched down in front of him, smiling widely. "Don't worry, Gabriel. We'll take good care of Fiona. And we have a son that can protect her, like you have!"

Adult Fiona snorted at the statement.

The boy's amber eyes darted from the couple to Miss Jenkins as realization sunk in. "No. *No.*" Tears streamed down his chubby cheeks.

"Give Fiona a hug, Gabriel."

"Gabe." The little girl squeezed the boy, and he hugged back silently. Fiona looked up as her adoptive mother grasped her tiny hand. She waved at him with the other as they headed for the door.

Miss Jenkins embraced her ward as the memory faded.

"I cried for three months after the Coopers took you." He nervously flexed the fingers of his free hand.

"I knew your name then." Gabe nodded at statement. "You remembered who we were though?"

"The entire time. Trust me, it *did not* help me get adopted."

"Why aren't you ready for church?" a middle-aged woman questioned a teenaged Gabe. "In this house we attend church every Sunday, rain or shine. You are expected to do so."

"I'm sorry, ma'am, but I do not go to church. Your god is a fairy tale."

Fiona tried unsuccessfully to hold back a snigger. "I thought the same thing growing up. Went through the motions to keep the Coopers happy."

"Every foster child we've had in this house has gone to mass with us, no question." The woman's mousy brown bob shook as the memory faded.

"That was my fourth foster family. I didn't get placed anywhere after. I aged out." His full lips flashed their self-assured smile. "I was luckier than most who age out…for obvious reasons. I joined the Army."

A corner of Fiona's mouth lifted. "I always liked you in uniform."

"Exactly my thought. The country needed warriors. And this time they let women enlist. I thought it would be my best chance to find you." He paused. "I didn't know you couldn't remember. You threatened to forget."

Frustration furrowed her brow. "I remembered you when I was adopted."

His eyes rolled up to the right as he thought. "I always thought of that. When I walked into the Purple Bear the first time, I fully expected you to run up and kiss me."

She looked him up and down. "I'm not saying I didn't want to, but it wasn't because I remembered you." She bumped him gently with her shoulder.

Gabe's eyes lit up as he chuckled, shaking his head. "You forgot me. You forgot *you*. I needed a plan B."

"My dreams."

"*Our* dreams. It was how we found one another the last times, but we need to be fairly physically close to one another. Once I got to the State Police detachment in Elkins, I was near enough to share dreams with you." He turned his head and met her eyes. "You've always wondered about your lucid dreams." She bowed her head in agreement. "Our dreams were our playground. We fell asleep each night and met on the shore, then walked into the ocean, into another world we imagined. Or—possibly —places in the other universes we created. I don't know. Regardless, I knew I could find you in dreams." He shrugged. "It took me a while to get up the courage to say the same things to you in the waking world. I wasn't certain how you would react. I didn't want you to think you were losing your mind."

"I'm not going to lie, it was odd." Fiona gently chewed the inside of her cheek. "Why would I want to forget me, Gabe?"

His eyes searched the ether. "After we destroyed this world a few times, we started to have nightmares. We lacked our usual control during them. You had nightmares worse than I did." His Adam's apple bobbed as he swallowed hard. "The atrocities we witnessed, the pain of our deaths in the world. You woke up screaming, sobbing, wanting to forget, *threatening* to forget. Threatening to leave this world to its own devices the next time." Gabe stared down at the pearl-gray mist swirling at his feet.

Guilt lowered Fiona's eyes. An apology caught in her throat as the haze cleared into another memory.

Eight

"Let's move on, Fiona." Gabe's voice cracked as he tugged her hand.

A flurry of activity came into view as the haze cleared.

"Fiona! Fiona? Where are you?" An injured Gabe, clad in a combat uniform, struggled against the medic trying to remove his body armor.

"Fucking hold still, LaCroix! Jesus fucking Christ!"

Gabe pushed the medic back violently and sat up halfway, blood trickling from his nostrils.

"Hold him *still*, Jackson." The other medic ripped open Gabe's sleeve and jabbed him with a syringe.

Medic Jackson eased Gabe onto his back as the sedative calmed him. "Fi-Fiona. Where are you?" Terrified amber orbs searched the dusty madness.

The other medic patted his shoulder. "We'll get you home to Fiona, soldier."

Fiona planted her feet as Gabe made one last attempt to pull her along. "You were injured in Afghanistan."

All the memories of the day shared a similar surrealism save this one. Fiona *knew* she and Gabe were before her in all of them, but they were Fionas and Gabes of past times. The Gabe in this scene was the man next to her; the man who searched for her; the man who went to war to find her.

She let go of Gabe's hand and moved closer to the injured soldier.

"Blood pressure's dropping, sir."

"Fi?" Lids closed half way over the soldier's glassy eyes.

"*Fuck*. He's bleeding somewhere. Goddamn sand niggers." The medic turned to search his bag. "*C'mon*. Stay with me, LaCroix."

Fiona's fingers itched to touch the Gabe of memory, but she knew she couldn't. "How were you injured?" she asked, looking up at her guide.

"My convoy hit an IED." He flexed his fingers absentmindedly. "I felt myself dying. I could see the Forest. I fought with everything I had, clawed my way back."

The soldier's back arched as he inhaled sharply. "Fi. Fuck."

The medic working on him turned and grinned. "That's right, soldier, you just keep on thinking of her and stay with me. We're going to get you home to her, LaCroix."

Pale mist surrounded them again.

Fiona returned to Gabe's side and squeezed his hand. Her brain scrambled for words. An apology seemed the only appropriate response, but nothing came to her lips.

Gabe eyed her quietly. "In all honesty, I believe it was better that you weren't there. I would have let myself die had you been. I knew I needed to survive to find you and fix this."

⇛⇝

The funk of sleep lifted slowly as Fiona sat up. She brushed a ruddy lock of hair from her face, sighing.

Gabe stretched his muscular arms above his head and studied her. His face fell. "You're still not remembering *you.*"

She buried her face in her hands. The memories played like movies to her, and, though she co-starred, she couldn't recall herself living the lives of the forest spirit, the leather-clad warrior, the nurse, or the Blitz-era Brit. Fiona Albright's life was one of escape and survival: fleeing her abusive sibling, living on the streets, and finally whittling a place for herself in Laurel Springs.

One thing she knew for certain: She didn't want Gabe meeting whatever violence awaited him in the West Side.

"How did you find me?" she asked, uncovering her face.

Gabe rubbed the dusky stubble on his cheeks. "I persuaded Miss Jenkins to tell me more about the Coopers. Strictly speaking, it was illegal as hell, but my brush with death swayed her." The tawny eyes shifted toward the ceiling as he remembered. "I thought she'd never stop crying, the poor woman. She apologized for not being able to keep us together, for not being able to find me a home." He shook his head sadly. "After talking to your adoptive family, I was glad, on one hand, they didn't adopt me as well."

Fiona's stomach twisted as she recalled her brother, Justin: the extra attention he paid her as puberty hit; the way his ice blue eyes bored into hers; not being able to tell her mother and father without fear. She hugged her knees to her chest.

Gabe reached out to touch her but pulled his hand back at the last second, a moue on his face. "I still can't touch you." He exhaled heavily. "If we grew up together, I have no doubts about you remembering." His jaw firmed. "Though, I would have killed Justin the first time he looked at you wrong."

She turned her head and eyed him. "I did a decent job defending myself."

Gabe met her gaze. "The Coopers explained to me what happened. How you ran away. Your brother confessed to raping you. The broken nose and, um, other damage."

She swallowed hard and turned her head so her long hair covered her face. "I told him one more time and he'd be sorry. I couldn't stay there any longer." She'd almost laughed at the stunned look in the boy's eyes as he lost consciousness. "No one expects the left hook from a righty."

The trooper *huh'd*. "Not even me." He winced. "The other stuff…"

"The hunting knife to his manhood? Killing him wouldn't have taught him the lesson." Figuring it to be her only line of defense on the streets, she had brought the knife along when she fled. It now sat hidden between her mattress and boxspring.

Gabe shrugged. "I'd still like to get my hands on him," he admitted. "Anyway, your mother and father held out hope that you'd come back. They wanted more than anything to apologize to you and to see you again, Fiona."

A tinge of guilt pierced her heart. Bud and Leslie Cooper had never left her in need of affection or encouragement. Both had eagerly watched her blossom into an intelligent, beautiful teenager. They bragged about her every chance they found, making Fiona's creamy skin glow in embarrassment. She retreated into herself when Justin's abuse started, convinced, with the aid of his lies, the loving parents would send her back to the group home if she ever told them.

"The police never found a trace of you. They figured you dead, like so many other runaways. But me, I knew better." The cocky smile momentarily spread over his face. "You know how to survive, Fiona. It's ingrained in you. Whatever we are—spirits or gods—we survive." He paused. "They all figured you ran towards New York City, but they don't know you like I do. You wanted the forest and the wild. That's where you thrive! So I took my chances with the wild, wonderful state of West Virginia and enrolled in the police academy." He rose, turning to her. "I'm honestly at a loss now, though. I don't know how else to get your memory back."

"Don't go, Gabe, please," she begged.

"You know I have to. I'll be back when I can, to keep you safe." He knelt down in front of her and motioned for her to lift her chin. "Keep your door locked. Be cautious at the shop. It's not close to the rioting, but don't trust anyone, except Jaime. Take that knife with you, too." He headed toward the door.

Fiona nodded and followed him. "Stay safe, Gabriel LaCroix," she ordered, bringing her eyes to his.

He gave her a half smile and tipped his wide brim to her as he left.

Nine

"Is Gabe out there? One of those guys in riot gear?" Jaime asked as Fiona stared at the shop's television. He placed a hand between her shoulder blades, knowing instinctively where her tension lingered.

"Yes," she answered hoarsely.

As days passed, the rioting increased. People came by bus from other towns and cities to join; some referred to them as professional rioters, though Fiona saw them as rabble-rousers and preferred to call them assholes. West Side businesses faced looters and fires. Police stood with imposing German shepherds, shields, and batons to keep the crowds in line as bottles and other garbage flew in their direction.

Issues even arose in other cities. People staged protests in larger areas. In places, police officers were ambushed on traffic stops.

When she returned home each evening, she avoided turning on her small television, but the images haunted her nonetheless. Where had Gabe been in the crowds?

Had he stayed safe? What if he got killed? What if she never remembered herself?

A soft knock at her door each evening washed away the day's fears. "I don't want to leave you alone. That is, if you don't mind a houseguest," Gabe stated the first night. He always gave her a lopsided smile before heading to shower off the day's dirt and his disgust. But she wondered how much of his stay was due to him not wanting to be alone.

Each night, Fiona snuck into the living room to study his sleeping form while willing her lost memory to return. She thanked the moon for illuminating the features she found so striking: the straight nose, full lips, smooth brow, and dark lashes of his closed eyes. His gentle, steady breathing lulled her to her own slumber. When they met in the dream world, they silently sat next to one another staring at the breaking waves. He never questioned her presence in the room when he rose in the morning.

"I know he's safe, Fi." Jaime petted her hair as he gazed around the empty shop, sighing. "It's pointless being here, isn't it? C'mon. I'll lock up and drive you home." A grunt left his throat. "Race riots are *not* good for business," he observed, locking the door.

"Who would have guessed?" she joked as she switched off the TV and headed to the kitchen to grab her keys and wallet.

Both items fell from her fingers as the glass shattered in the room behind her.

"Get the fuck out of my shop, sons 'a bitches."

Fiona peeked around the door frame. Jaime stood his ground as two men walked through the broken door.

The first, a tall, wiry Caucasian rubbing snuff, pushed him roughly, but failed to move the larger man. "What're ya gonna do, faggot?"

Her boss's shove knocked the man to the floor.

The other intruder, a short black man, picked up the brick they had used to break the window; he studied Jaime, then smashed the brick on the back of his head. Jaime's six foot frame crumpled to the ground.

Fiona held her breath, realizing her friend was dead.

"Motherfucker," the white man grumbled, kicking Jaime's still body.

"*Shit.*" She turned back to the kitchen, scurrying to a low cabinet and cramming herself in. Her arms hugged her knees as she fought to calm her breathing.

The register *ching'd*. "Fag was hardly ever here alone."

Her heart thudded painfully as she heard a boot jangle her keys. *Fuck. Fuck.*

Fluorescent light blinded her as the looter yanked her from her cabinet sanctuary. "Ohhh. The pretty one." His fingers dug into the soft flesh of her upper arm as he pulled her to her feet. "Remember me?"

Fiona glared up at him as he spat a wad of snuff onto the clean linoleum. Two months prior, Scotty Crane had grabbed her wrist as she handed a customer a coffee. *Why not just yank my hair like we're in kindergarten? What every girl wants: an abusive, juvenile ass.* Just as she had felt the fingers of her left hand balling up, Jaime came to the rescue. Her boss banned him from the cafe for assaulting her.

"What're gonna do without that fag to protect ya, sweetie?" He grabbed a skein of her hair a turned her face upward.

A growing ball of sadness and dread roiled in her belly. *Jaime.*

The other man shuffled over to study Fiona, tugging up his sagging jeans. "She ain't that special, Scotty. Huh. I get 'er when you're done."

"The fuck either of you will," she mumbled.

Scotty jerked her head harder. "Shut up." His palm stung as it made contact with her cheek, then the smack of tobacco and cheap beer assailed her tastebuds as he forced his tongue between her lips. He let go of her hair in favor of her breasts while his hand tore at the button of her denim shorts.

Fiona pushed him back before Scotty could get his hand down her shorts. She head-butted him as he moved back toward her.

The black man laughed as his partner spat out a front tooth. "Shut the *fuck up*, Derek," he slurred, wiping blood from his mouth. "Motherfucking cunt." A hand slick with blood and saliva wrapped around her throat and slammed her head against the tiled wall.

Tiny ballerinas of light pirouetted in front of Fiona's eyes. She dug her fingernails into Scotty's wrist, his fingers tightening around her windpipe. "There. Now you're quiet." Her attacker's other hand grabbed her breast and violently pinched her nipple. His fingers scratched down her body and up the leg of her shorts.

I've let Gabe down. Gabe.

The world in front of her shrank as she felt her fingers slip from Scotty's wrist.

War drums. Mmm. There are always war drums, she thought fondly as the slowing booms of her heart filled her brain.

Majestic oaks hundreds of feet high replaced the angry face in front of her.

❧❦

The left hook threw the rapist back five feet. A gob of snuff and blood left his mouth and hit the floor with a wet *swhack.*

Fiona sucked down lungfuls of oxygen, her chest heaving, as a universe expanded in her head. *Ten times. We've destroyed this sorry excuse for a world ten times, Gabe and I.*

We've died for this world. Her head moved side to side, vertebrae popping softly, as she recalled the peaceful morphine sleep and the white hot pain of being impaled. *Not this time. We fix it this time.* Her breathing slowed as she thought of her consort: the musky, clean animal fragrance of his body; his smooth skin against her own; the sounds he made as he slid in and out of her. *Gabriel.* Then the heartbreaking susurrus met her ears as the rush of blood eased; she sighed as she heard the world keening. *How could I not hear you crying? I left Gabe to listen to you alone.*

As Scotty charged her, she smirked, remembering the hunting knife at the small of her back. The blade slid smoothly through the tender flesh behind the man's chin. He fell to the floor, a heap of thrashing limbs, spraying dark blood on the cabinets and floor. *This is the first time I've had to kill here,* she realized mournfully as the body grew still.

Derek stood gaping as his accomplice's life ended in a pool of crimson. He grabbed a knife from the counter and rushed her.

The report of gunfire echoed in the shop as Derek fell.

Fiona's head swiveled to her right as the trooper lowered his Glock. Relief and joy spread warmly through her as she studied the black anti-riot suit. *My Gabe in uniform.* Armor-like guards protected his shoulders, arms, thighs, and shins from the destructive mob. A shielded helmet covered his head, and a baton hung at his side. Though intimidating to others, the riot gear sent a stab of desire through her. "Gabe," she sighed, replacing the knife.

He lifted his face shield as she approached. "Fiona?"

She took his face in her hands and kissed him deeply, savoring the taste of his tongue on hers.

A laugh shook his chest before he stepped back from her. "You remember you."

Fiona smiled. "I do." She wrapped her fingers in his and lead him to the shattered door, but stopped, knelt down next to Jaime, and turned him over with care. "I think you knew what I am, Jaime. Thank you for trying to protect me," she whispered, wiping the blood from his light hair and closing his green eyes. Fiona leaned in, planting a kiss on his forehead, before rising. "I'm sick of this universe, Gabriel LaCroix."

He nodded, dropping the face shield. "Your place is closer."

Ten

Fiona watched Gabe throw his body guards and helmet in a nearby chair before turning to latch the locks on the door.

Her eyes roamed over the remaining black uniform as she turned to him. She slid closer and cupped his cheek. The prickly stubble of his five o'clock shadow gently scratched her palms; it was something his smooth skin lacked in the Forest, so Fiona let her eyelids slip shut and enjoyed the sensation.

"As soon as I remembered, every nerve in me longed to touch you." She opened her eyes to his.

He moved her hand up to his mouth and lightly kissed her fingertips. His other hand moved to her shoulder; she tilted her head back with a contented breath, realizing just how much she missed his touch. The back of his fingers softly grazed the darkening bruises on her creamy flesh. "Is this how you remembered?"

She barely dipped her head in response. "I could hear the slow *boom-boom* of war drums and thought, 'Of course!

They always have some little drummer pounding away for them to kill to!' Then our beautiful forest started materializing…and I realized the sound wasn't drums."

He leaned in and grazed her neck with his lips, sending an electric tingle through her body. His face moved back up, and his amber eyes searched her cerulean irises.

"How could I ever want to forget, when we come from all that beauty?" She slowly unbuttoned his shirt. "Everything came back to me in a flood. All the times we successfully destroyed this universe. The two times I died here…you died here. The feel of you against me." Her hand caressed Gabe's cotton-covered chest, smiling as his nipples hardened under her fingers. "I fought my way back. I was wrong to want to forget." She lifted herself onto the balls of her feet and pressed her lips to his. "This is who we are. This is our responsibility. We cannot let the suffering of this world continue." A sense of duty tightened her stomach.

"My Fiona," he sighed, sliding his hands down her sides. One hand snuck around the front of her body to unbutton her shorts; with little coaxing, they slipped over the firm roundness of her backside and down her bare legs. A delighted shudder trembled through Fiona as a finger grazed the soft skin between her hips. His hands continued down her body and pulled her in close. Gabe buried his face in her tresses and breathed in. "It was torture not touching you, Fi."

"I'm sorry I made things so difficult." Gabe's hardness pressing against her conquered her rising guilt. A warm tingle spread through her belly. She gently moved back to unbuckle his belt then slid down to her knees, taking the trousers with her. "My beautiful, Gabriel," she breathed studying his manhood. "How could I *ever* want to forget you?" She tilted her head up to meet his eyes, then took him into her mouth. She inhaled the scent of his body, his soft, warm fragrance. Her hands deftly unzipped his boots while her mouth moved up and down.

A muffled giggle escaped Fiona's mouth as Gabe's fingers tugged gently at her hair. "Please, Fi," he mumbled. He slipped his hands under her arms and lifted her to her feet. She wrapped her legs around his waist and greedily brought her mouth to his, taking back what she'd forced herself to give up. He kicked off the boots as he carried her toward the bedroom.

The sounds of voices and breaking glass in the street below halted Gabe's progress. He looked at Fiona, confusion and worry in his eyes. "There wasn't protesting on this side of the city." He finished carrying Fiona to the bed and set her down.

He started to turn toward the window, but she pulled him down next to her. She searched his eyes and kissed his forehead. "They know what's coming. After all these times they can sense it, but they can't *stop* it." She slid the shirt down his shoulders and off his muscular arms, hearing the world's soft, pained moans.

Gabe grinned. "Pay no heed to the rabble," he laughed pulling his T-shirt over his head.

Fiona's fingers caressed the black antlers as he pulled her cami off. She laid back, pulling him on top of her, adoring the reverent way he studied her bare breasts. Her back arched as his tongue traced the vines and flowers decorating her skin. She closed her eyes and played with his short raven hair as his lips brushed down to her hardening nipples. A tiny cry escaped her as he grazed one with his teeth.

A husky laugh answered her as he moved down the soft flesh of her midriff. He paused before he reached her womanhood and ran the tip of his nose between the shallow valley created by the hills of her pelvis. Her body pressed up toward his face. He pinned her down playfully and let the tip of his tongue linger right below the Titian trail.

"Don't make me beg, Gabe, please." Her heart threatened to burst as she squirmed under his palms.

Gabe glanced up at her with a raised eyebrow. Fiona bit her lip, pleading with her eyes.

He kept his gaze locked on hers while he slid his hands to her backside and his mouth between her lips. His gaze shifted down as his tongue lent itself to the task at hand.

Fiona's nails dug into his naked shoulders, leaving bright red scratches, as her lover's mouth indulged her. The tip of Gabe's tongue teased, bringing her nearly to the crest, then cruelly moved to another spot. She lost control of herself and held his face between her thighs as a tsunami of white-hot pleasure washed over her. She released her consort and hugged herself as the wave ebbed. "Gabe…"

The man slid up her body and kissed her with soaked lips. "I *am* good." He gave her a cocky smile as he laid his head down on her glistening midriff.

Fiona ran fingers through Gabe's short hair and listened to his breathing as he gently stroked her skin. She closed her eyes, dozing.

❧

Fiona's eyes snapped open. "Oh. I understand now…"

She pulled Gabe's face up to hers and brushed her lips against his. His amber gaze met hers. "I know why we came here as children." She felt the threat of tears as his head tilted questioningly. "We never understood, Gabe. We came here, and we never really saw the suffering. We did our duty and left it. We didn't know the pain, even when we heard the world crying."

Gabe brushed stray tears from her cheeks. "What do you mean?"

"It needed *us* to suffer with it. It tried to make us suffer by separating us, but—oh—we were too good. Think about it: We were never farther from one another than this time. As children we had no control…and that's what the universe wanted. The horrors we experienced." She cupped his cheek. "Abandonment, abuse, war, loss, violence. The world screamed, but we didn't fully understand the horror *until now*."

He shuddered, realization spreading over his face.

Their heads turned as one as the crack of a shotgun echoed from the street. Muffled screams met their ears.

"Holy shit," he muttered in disgust.

Fiona took his face in her hands. "This universe has grown like a tumor. Larger and more malignant each time it comes back. We end the pain for good this time." She pressed her lips to his and rolled him onto his back.

Fiona's lips showered his closed eyelids and warm cheeks, then moved down to his neck. She lingered a moment on the throbbing pulse there, appreciating the flow of life rushing through his body, before softly licking his earlobe.

His fingers wove themselves into the waves of her hair as a throaty moan left him. "Fiona," he prayed as her head moved lower.

She propped herself up on her elbows and tenderly traced the antlers with a fingertip before playing with the sensitive skin crowning his nipples. She listened to his soft grunts and moans with a satisfied smile.

This was how their life was meant to be. There would be no more of this universe. Just pleasure back in the forest.

Gabe's hands released her hair as she eased down between his muscular thighs. Another plea left him as her lips enveloped his manhood. She slid her mouth down the smooth flesh and let her fingers tickle where they could. "Please, Fiona."

Fiona answered his prayers. She slid back up and straddled her consort, slipping him inside her body with a long moan. "You never disappoint me, Gabriel," she breathed, feeling him fill her completely.

The sounds of madness below increased as their bodies glided together. A woman screamed as another gunshot reverberated. Stern voices raised in anger and fear as glass shattered. Sharp barks and growls came from the police dogs. Barely audible dull thuds marked the falling of both officers and protesters.

Fiona bit her lip and rode as Gabe pressed her harder onto him, shutting her ears to the sounds outside. She closed her eyes, reveling in the delicate pinching pain of his fingers digging into her hips. Her cerulean eyes opened to his amber ones, and she grinned at the ethereal vibrating energy rippling around them.

Gabe's hand found the small of her back, holding himself in her body as he rolled them over with a grunt. Fiona wrapped her legs around his waist, pulling him in even deeper, and dug her fingers into his forearms as he moved harder and faster against her lithe frame.

Her eyes slid shut again as their cries drowned out all other noises.

His mouth found hers, biting her bottom lip. "Fi," he panted, nuzzling her arched neck.

"Gabe." She licked her parted lips, nodding.

Searing heat and bright scarlet light filled the world as the lovers climaxed.

Epilogue

Sunlight stole through branches, desperate to wake the slumbering pair.

Fiona's eyes opened to the oaks gazing down on her and Gabe. *Home. Finally.* Her body felt light again, her heart contented. She rolled on her side and met her lover's gaze. A corner of his mouth quirked up, then he planted a kiss on her forehead.

She gave him a coy smile and ran a finger down his bare chest, then moved in close to his ear. "Catch me, Gabe," she whispered before taking off down a game trail.

Gabe sat up and grinned in his cocky way, adjusting the antlers on his cropped raven hair. "Three…two…one," he counted, gifting his consort a head-start. He popped up and trotted after Fiona, mischief filling his amber eyes.

The End

Alternate Ending

"Do you think we ended it for good this time?" Gabe asked, running the back of his hand along her doe skin vest.

Fiona took his hand gently and eased it over the emerging bump of her belly. His amber eyes widened in mingled fear and joy. "I think we ended one thing to begin another."

About the Author

S.L. Baron isn't a full-time writer but keeps wishing she could quit her day job. She's been scribbling down stories since she was a small child, and she's glad the evidence of those stories no longer exists. After reading Anne Rice's *Interview With The Vampire*, she found her Muse. She's been obsessed with vampires and other types of immortals ever since. When she's not writing about her own Children of the Night, she reads all she can get her hands on about these and other supernatural creatures.

S.L. grew up near the shore in the New Jersey Pinelands but lives in West Virginia. She graduated from West Virginia University with a Bachelor of Arts in psychology. Keeping her company is her partner in crime, Tim, and three insane cats.

You can follow her on Facebook @AuthorSLBaron, on Instagram @authorslbaron, and at her website, authorslbaron.com. If you enjoyed this book, please leave a review on Amazon, Barnes and Noble, Goodreads, and anywhere else you can spread the love!